A Big Fat Enormous Lie

by Marjorie Weinman Sharmat

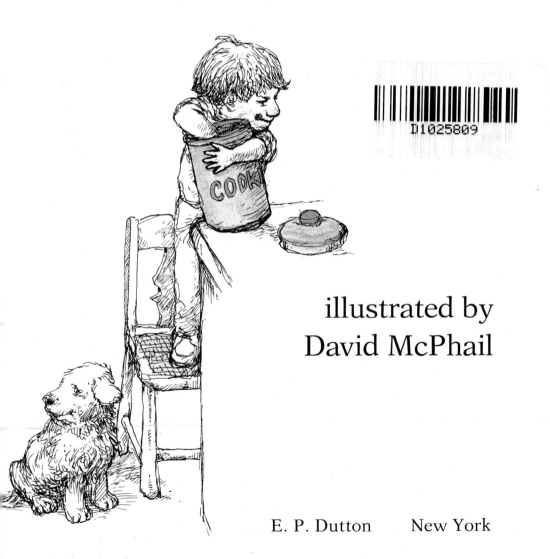

illustrated by
David McPhail

E. P. Dutton   New York

Text copyright © 1978 by Marjorie Weinman Sharmat
Illustrations copyright © 1978 by David McPhail

All rights reserved.

Unicorn is a registered trademark of E. P. Dutton.

Library of Congress number 77-15645
ISBN 0-525-44242-1

Published in the United States by E. P. Dutton,
2 Park Avenue, New York, N.Y. 10016

Published simultaneously in Canada by
Fitzhenry & Whiteside Limited, Toronto

Editor: Ann Durell   Designer: Meri Shardin

Printed in Hong Kong by South China Printing Co.
First Unicorn Edition 1986   W
10 9 8 7 6 5 4 3 2

for my sons, Craig and Andrew,
with big fat enormous love

I told a lie.
A big fat enormous gigantic lie.
Father asked me if I ate the jar of cookies.
I said no.

But I did.
And I told a lie.
I could have told the truth.
I could have said "I ate the cookies."
But my father would have gotten mad

And my mother would have gotten mad.

And my sister.

Now I'm sorry I ate them.
And I'm sorry I lied.
And now I'm stuck with my lie.

I could talk to it, maybe.
"Lie, go away. Scram. I'll give you a dime
if you never come back."

It's still here.

"Look, Lie. I don't want you and I don't like you. And I can't see you, so maybe you don't exist. You don't exist, Lie. You are nothing. Nothing. Nothing. NOTHING!

So why are you still here?
I can't see you, but I know you're
getting bigger and bigger.
You are enormous, Lie."

"You are enormous and gigantic and you
are a big-fat. You have a mushy head

and a runny nose and a bulging stomach.
You are ugly, Lie."

"And dumb. You are the dumbest. I bet you
can't spell your own name. Try it.

L-Y, L-I, L-Y-E, L-I-I-I, L-Y-Y-Y. All wrong."

"You are L-I-E, and you're dumb, and I'm

too smart for you. So how did I get
stuck with you?"

"Couldn't you go bother somebody else?
Somebody really mean and rotten. Not a
nice kid like me.

Is that you sitting on my stomach, Lie?
That hurts. Get off. Get off.
Okay, Lie. I give up.''

"Father! Mother!

I lied to you. I know who ate the cookies.
Someone I like very much ate the cookies. He
sort of ate one and then he sort of ate another
and then he sort of ate another.
He sort of ate all the cookies in the jar."

"Yes. I sort of ate them. Me. Your son.

Are you going to do anything about it,
Father? Mother?"

"You two will discuss it?
Okay."
Okay!

My lie has gone. Maybe it left to bother
somebody else.

Maybe it's halfway around the world by now.
Maybe it's swimming in the ocean

or marooned on a beach waiting to be rescued.

Maybe it's lost in a big city

or a forest, wishing it hadn't left a
nice kid like me.
But it won't come back to me.
I don't have it anymore.

And that's the absolute and total truth.